The Clatterbangs Go To Town

By Neil Gaw

Illustrated By Jose Ohi

The Clatterbangs were awful
The worst people you could find

Rude, noisy and terrible
Not one bit of them was kind

Four of them altogether
There was the Father and the Mother

Kerry was their daughter
And Jerry, her little brother

And last but not least was Jerry
Eating chocolate wherever he goes

His little belly had gotten so big
He could hardly see his toes

The Clatterbangs Go To Town

By Neil Gaw

ISBN: 9781654962265

Look Out For Other Books In The Clatterbang Series!

Printed in Poland
by Amazon Fulfillment
Poland Sp. z o.o., Wrocław